This book belongs to

....

....

A catalogue record for this book is available from the British Library
Published by Ladybird Books Ltd.
A Penguin Company
80 Strand, London, WC2R 0RL, England
Penguin Books Australia Ltd, 250 Camberwell Road,
Camberwell, Victoria 3124, Australia
New York, Canada, India, New Zealand, South Africa

7 9 10 8

ISBN-13: 978-1-84422-407-4

Printed in China

Happy Birthday,
Spot

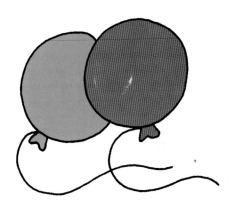

Eric Hill

Spot woke up happy and excited.
Today was his birthday!
He rushed down to his breakfast.

"Happy birthday, Spot!" said
Sally and Sam. "You've got a
lot of cards!"

Spot opened his cards and then had breakfast. It was fun having a birthday, and his friends were coming for tea later on.

"Are you making a cake for my birthday, Mum?" asked Spot. "Yes," said Sally. "A very special one. Would you like to help me?"

"Yes, please!" said Spot. "I'd like to do the icing – all different colours!"
"Alright, let's start," said Sally.

9

Sally started to make the cake.
Ginger cat wanted to help as well.

"I don't think we need your help,
Ginger cat," said Sally. "But you
can help me clean up afterwards."

Sam came into the kitchen.
"It's so nice outside," he said.
"We should have your party in
the garden, Spot."

"Good idea, Dad!" said Spot.
"I'll help you to get everything
ready."

Spot and Sam hung balloons and streamers all over the garden.
It looked very colourful.

"This is my best birthday ever!" said Spot.

Spot finished in the garden and went to the kitchen. There was a lovely smell.

"You can do the icing now, Spot," said Sally.

"And when you've done that, you can put the candles on the cake. Then we're nearly ready."

As Spot put the last candle on the cake, he heard the doorbell ring. He ran to the door and there was Tom, Helen and Steve holding brightly wrapped presents.

"Happy birthday, Spot!" they all said.

Spot couldn't wait to open his presents!

There was a new ball from Steve and a big box of crayons from Tom. Helen had brought Spot a jigsaw with a picture of a farm.

"Thank you for my presents!"
said Spot, giving each of his
friends a big hug. "They're just
what I wanted!"

Then Spot and his friends went out to the garden to play their favourite games until it was time for tea.

Sally brought out all the food and everyone put on party hats.

"Sausages!" said Tom. "They are my favourites!"

"And jelly and ice cream!"
said Steve.
"And wait till you see the cake!"
said Spot. "I helped to make it."

At last Sally and Sam brought in the birthday cake – with a special surprise on top!

"Look!" Helen exclaimed. "It's a little Spot, made of icing sugar!"

"And I thought I was the one who did the icing," laughed Spot.

Sam lit the candles and everyone sang, "Happy Birthday."
Spot was very happy.

With one great big puff, Spot blew out every single candle. Then he closed his eyes to make his birthday wish.
Everyone cheered.
"What did you wish for, Spot?" asked Helen.
"I can't tell you," said Spot.
"If I did, it wouldn't come true!"

Everyone cheered again.
"Happy birthday, Spot! We hope
you get your wish!"

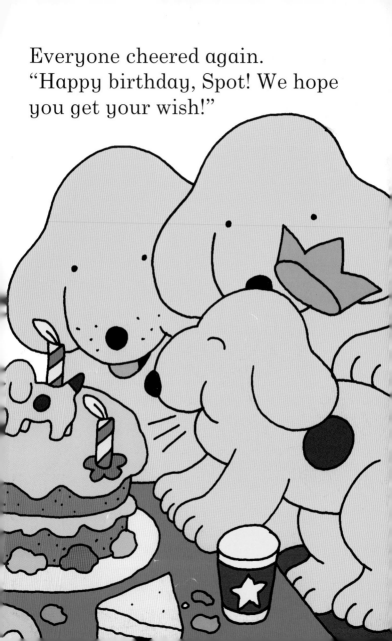

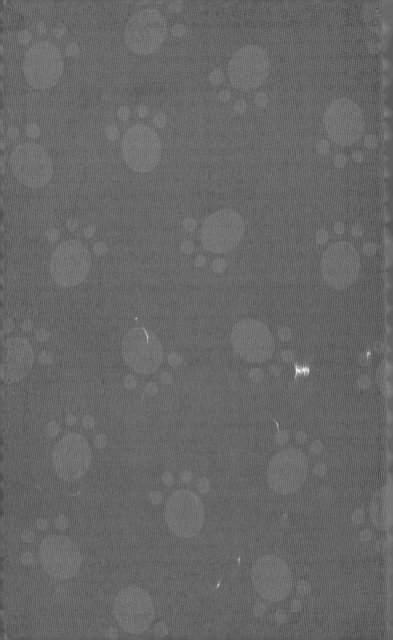